THE FLOWER FAIRIES

STICKER
ACTIVITY
BOOK

with illustrations by
CICELY MARY BARKER

◆

WARNE

ABOUT THIS BOOK

◆

This book is about the natural world of the Flower Fairies. There are ideas
on how to plan a flower trail, and recipes for a flower fairy picnic to
take with you. After your flower trail, you can record your findings
in your Flower Fairies seasonal nature chart. You can also learn how to use
pressed and dried flowers to create your own pretty framed
Flower Fairy nature collage.

Best of all, in the middle of this book you will find three beautifully
illustrated background scenes and a sheet of flower and fairy stickers to go
with them. To use the sticker section, open the book in the middle and lay
it out flat. Ask an adult to help you open the staples. Carefully remove the
sticker section and close the staples again. Now you can peel individual
stickers off the backing sheet and place your fairy and flower stickers on any
of the three seasonal backgrounds. You will be able to use and reuse the
stickers - but do not put them down on anything else, as they might stick!
Be careful also not to stick them to your clothes or the carpet because they
will pick up fluff and won't then stick to the book. When you have finished
playing with the stickers, replace them on the backing sheet for
safe-keeping until you are ready to use them again.
Have fun!

The Flower Fairies

◆

Cicely Mary Barker created a collection of Flower Fairies for every season and a poem about each fairy. In this book you'll find a Spring and Summer scene, an Autumn scene, and a Winter scene, and your task is to position each fairy sticker in its rightful place. Here are some helpful hints about some of the fairies you'll find in this book, based on the charming fairy poems.

Fairies of the Spring and Summer

Pear Blossom is one of the first fairies to wake with the Spring, Herb Twopence creeps along the ground, and the young Strawberry Fairy bears his basket of delicious fruit for the Queen and all of her court to eat. Pretty dancing Columbine and little Pansy come with their brightly-coloured flowers while the Zinnia Fairy tends her tall pink blooms. The orange flowers of the Nasturtium Fairy last all summer long but the sweet-scented Rose is the 'best and dearest flower that grows'.

Fairies of the Autumn

All the pretty blossom that came in the spring has borne fruit by Autumn time. The Crab-Apple Fairy holds out her dress to collect her fairy-fruit. The Elm Tree Fairy sits in his tree, keeping watch over the land, while the Ash Tree Fairy with her seeds like bunches of keys, dances along a branch. As the weather turns colder, the Hawthorn Fairy comes with his dark red berries to feed the hungry birds.

Fairies of the Winter

While most plants lose their leaves in the cold winter and lie dormant until the spring, the winter fairies waken to bring colour to the snowy landscape. The Box Tree keeps its dark green leaves all year round, and the sprightly Holly Fairy comes with his scarlet berries to decorate hedgerows and woods.

The Rush-Grass Fairy lives near marshland and warns travellers not to stray from the path, while the Winter Jasmine Fairy tends his bright yellow flowers all through the cold weather. But most special of all, the Christmas Tree Fairy flies down and alights on top of every decorated Christmas tree.

A Nature Collage

◆

This is the Sweet Pea Fairy trying on a pretty bonnet for her baby sister. You can make this picture into a beautiful nature collage with a few dried or pressed leaves, flower petals and seeds.

YOU WILL NEED:
◆ blunt-ended scissors ◆ poster paints or felt-tip pens ◆ paper glue ◆ poppy seeds ◆ pressed flower petals and leaves or pot-pourri ◆ thin card 33 cm wide and 24 cm long (3 x 9.5 in) ◆ 1 metre of coloured ribbon ◆ sticky tape

1. Follow the dotted lines to cut out the picture and lay it on plenty of sheets of newspaper to keep the surfaces clean. Paint or colour the older Fairy's hair, stockings, shoes, and wings. Colour the plant stems green.

2. Dab a little glue on the older fairy's bodice. Shake the poppy seeds onto it, and allow to dry for a few minutes. Then shake the picture so that the loose poppy seeds fall off.

3. Collect together some pressed sweet pea petals and leaves. If you can't find Sweet Peas you can use another flower or some pot-pourri. Stick the petals and leaves on the picture with glue. If they are too big, use the scissors to shape them.

4. Glue your picture onto a piece of thin card. Ask an adult to help you puncture some holes through the picture, following the circles as a guide.

5. Now thread the coloured ribbon through alternate holes, starting from the left-bottom hole. When it reaches the other side, tie the two ends together in a pretty bow.

6. Stick a loop of ribbon to the top underside of the card with sticky tape and tie the ends together. Your beautiful picture is now ready to hang.

A Nature Crossword

◆

Test your knowledge of nature in this crossword.

1 *down.* Some people believe that if you hold this flower under your chin and it casts a yellow glow, it means you like butter!

2 *across.* This is the season when leaves fall from trees.

3 *across.* This little red fruit is delicious to eat and grows wild in hedges and woods in summer.

4 *down.* This sweet-smelling flower is usually sent as a message of love on St. Valentine's Day.

5 *across.* These flowers grow on the garden lawn and you can string them together to make a fairy necklace.

6 *down.* This is the colour of daffodils.

FIND THE FLOWER

◆

Here are the Pansy, Lily-of-the-Valley, Zinnia and Nasturtium Fairies. Can you follow the wiggly lines to help them find their flowers?

The Blackthorn Fairy

This is the Blackthorn fairy, decorating the hedges with her starry white blossoms after the long winter. That's why the cold days of March are sometimes called "Blackthorn Winter". Colour in the picture.

The White Bryony Fairy

This is the White Bryony Fairy adorning the hedges with her pretty strings of berries. See if you can find all the berries in the picture and colour them red.

A Nature Trail

◆

You can learn a lot about flowers simply by going on a nature walk. If you keep your eyes open you'll be really amazed at all the different places you can find plants growing - not just in your garden! Flowers grow in fields, woods, on the seashore and in hedgerows and meadows. You can find them growing in towns in between paving stones or in brick walls, in your playground and on wasteground.

Here are a few things you should take with you on your nature trail:

NOTEBOOK & PENCIL
For making quick sketches of the flowers you see, and describing them as well as you can. What colour is it? Does it have a scent? How many petals does it have?

MAGNIFYING GLASS
To help you see the small details of the flower which you can record in your notebook.

TAPE MEASURE
To check the height of the flower.

CLEAR PLASTIC BAGS
To keep your notebook dry in the rain and for collecting petals, leaves, seeds or common flowers.

DRAW A FLOWER MAP

Draw a map of the walk you went on, showing areas of woodland, rivers or streams, marshland or meadow. Mark the places where you saw flowers, butterflies, or bees, and name them if you can. This will give you an idea of where particular flowers like to grow.

LEAF AND BARK RUBBINGS

If you have ever examined the bark of a tree you will have noticed that it has a definite pattern. The pattern on one species of tree is quite unlike that on another, and can be a useful way of identifying the tree.

To make a bark rubbing, hold a piece of thick white paper against the bark and rub over it with the side of a pencil or crayon. If you can identify the tree, write its name under the bark rubbing. See how many different rubbings you can collect.

To make a leaf rubbing, place a leaf on a table with the veined side of the leaf uppermost. Place a sheet of thin paper over the leaf and rub over it with a pencil or crayon until the complete pattern of the leaf appears on the paper. Write down the name of the tree from which the leaf came.

PRESSING FLOWERS

When you get back from your walk, you can press the flowers and leaves you have collected. Place them between sheets of blotting paper, making sure that all the leaf and petal edges are spread out flat, and press them between the pages of a heavy book. You should leave them there for a few days before opening the book. You can glue the flowers to card and label them, or use them to make pretty cards and pictures to give to friends.

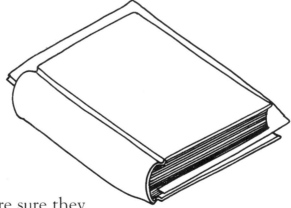

IMPORTANT

Please do not dig up flowers, and only pick them if you are sure they are common and there are lots of the same kind growing together. Never pick a flower which might be rare, even if you can see several of them growing. Always observe the country code - close gates behind you, never light fires, and make sure you take all your rubbish home with you.

REMEMBER - always tell an adult where you are going, and take a friend with you.

SPRING

The World is very old;
But year by year
It groweth new again
When buds appear.

The World is very old,
And sometimes sad;
But when the daisies come
The World is glad.

The World is very old;
But every Spring
It groweth young again,
And fairies sing.

IN SPRING I SAW

crocuses ☐ dandelions ☐

apple blossom ☐ deer ☐

daffodils ☐ rabbits ☐

bluebells ☐ lambs ☐

A PRESSED SPRING FLOWER
stick down a flower you found:

AUTUMN

An elfin rout,
With berries laden,
Throngs round about
A merry maiden.

Red-gold her gown;
Sun-tanned is she;
She wears a crown
Of bryony.

The sweet Spring came,
And lovely Summer:
Guess, then, her name—
This latest-comer!

IN AUTUMN I SAW

squirrels ☐ blackberries ☐

a flock of birds ☐ rose-hips ☐

daisies ☐ horse-chestnuts ☐

acorns ☐ Michaelmas daisies ☐

A FALLEN LEAF
stick down a leaf you found:

The
Strawberry
Fairy

The
Herb Twopence
Fairy

The
Pear Blossom
Fairy

The
Pansy
Fairy

The
Columbine
Fairy

The
Nasturtium
Fairy

The
Rose Fairy

The
Kingcup
Elf

The
Zinnia
Fairy

The
Box Tree
Fairy

The
Crab
Apple
Fairy

The
Elm
Tree
Fairy

The
Winter Jasmine
Fairy

The
Hawthorn
Fairy

The
Ash Tree
Fairy

The
Holly Fairy

The
Rush Grass
Fairy

The
Christmas
Tree
Fairy

CHART

SUMMER

The little darling, Spring,
Has run away;
The sunshine grew too hot
for her to stay.

She kissed her sister, Summer,
And she said:
"When I am gone, you must be
queen instead."

Now reigns the Lady Summer,
Round whose feet
A thousand fairies flock
with blossoms sweet.

IN SUMMER I SAW

buttercups ☐   roses ☐

forget-me-nots ☐   strawberries ☐

foxgloves ☐   butterflies ☐

honeysuckle ☐   bees ☐

A PRESSED SUMMER FLOWER
stick down a flower you found:

WINTER

Deep sleeps the Winter,
Cold, wet and grey;
Surely all the world is dead;
Spring is far away.

Wait! the world shall waken;
It is not dead, for lo,
The Fair Maids of February
Stand in the snow!

IN WINTER I SAW

snowdrops ☐   yew tree berries ☐

holly berries ☐   fir trees ☐

pine cones ☐   red robins ☐

winter jasmine ☐   foxes ☐

AN EVERGREEN LEAF
stick down a leaf you found:

Make A Daisy

◆

For a perfect gift, make a posy of these pretty paper daisies and present them with a matching card.

YOU WILL NEED:

4 squares of white crepe paper 18 cm x 18 cm (5 x 5 in) yellow crepe paper 10 cm x 10 cm (4 x 4 in)
◆ green crepe paper 10 cm x 2 cm (8 x 1 in) for stem ◆ square of green crepe paper 10 x 10 cm
(4 x 4in) for flower base ◆ blunt ended scissors ◆ 1 pipe cleaner ◆ paper glue ◆
tracing paper ◆ paperclips

1. Paperclip the squares of white crepe paper together.
2. Trace the petal template on the last page onto the top square, and cut out the petal shape.

3. Layer each square so that the petals overlap. Glue them together in the centre.

4. Tear off little pieces from the yellow crepe paper and roll them into balls. Stick them down to the middle of the white crepe paper flower.

5. Trace the petal base template on the inside back cover onto the square of green crepe paper, and cut out. Attach it to the underside of the flower head with glue.

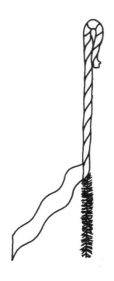

6. Wrap the strip of green crepe paper around the pipe cleaner, glueing the end down. Bend over the top of the pipe cleaner.

7. Stick the bent end of the pipe cleaner to the flower base with glue.
8. To make the leaves, cut out leaf shapes from the green crepe paper and stick them to the stem with glue.

Daisy Card

◆

Make a pretty daisy card to go with your paper flower.

YOU WILL NEED:

thin card in three colours: orange: 20 cm x 10 cm (8 x 4 in), yellow: 20 cm x 10 cm (8 x 4 in) and white: 5 cm x 5 cm (2 x 2 in) ◆ glue ◆ blunt-ended scissors

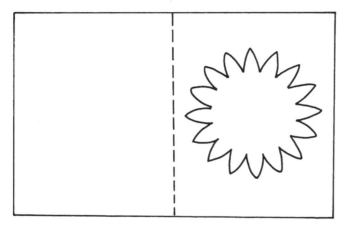

1. Fold the orange card in half. Draw a daisy shape on one side. Make a hole in the middle and carefully cut around the shape, being careful not to cut through the edges.

2. Cut a piece of white card to the same size as the folded orange card.

3. Spread some glue around the cut out daisy shape on the inside of the folded orange card and stick down the white card.

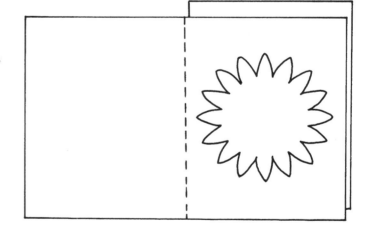

4. Cut out a circle from the yellow card and glue it to the centre of the daisy shape. Now write your message in the card.

SPOT THE DIFFERENCE

These two pictures of the Bugle Fairy look the same but if you look very
carefully you will see that there are some differences. Can you spot all the differences?
There are eight altogether.

THE SNAPDRAGON FAIRY

Here is the Snapdragon Fairy talking to a busy bee who has come to collect pollen from his bright flowers. Follow the numbers to help you colour in the picture.

1. Red   2. Dark Green   3. Yellow   4. Blue   5. Light Green   6. Orange   7. Black

The Columbine Fairy

Here is pretty pink Columbine dancing to the elfin piper's tune. Colour in the picture.

Jumbled Words

Four different flowers are growing in this garden. The label by each flower should tell you what the flowers are, but the letters have got jumbled up. Can you unjumble the letters and work out what the flowers are? The pictures of the flowers should give you a clue.

JOIN THE DOTS

I wonder which fairy this is? If you join the dots, following the numbers, you will find out.
When you have finished, you can colour the picture in.

A Fairy Picnic

◆

These fairy foods are fun to eat and make a perfect picnic to take with you on your nature trail.

Fairy Toadstools

Take the ingredients with you in a plastic container and assemble them into toadstools when you are ready to eat them.

INGREDIENTS:
- ◆ 2 hard boiled eggs, shelled ◆ wedge of cheddar cheese
- ◆ 2 tomatoes ◆ salad cress

1. Cut the cheese into short stalks.
2. Carefully cut the boiled eggs in half widthways and lay them cut-side down on top of the cheese stalks with a blob of mayonnaise. For red toadstools, use halved tomatoes instead of eggs.
3. Decorate the top of the eggs with blobs of salad cream or mayonnaise.
4. Arrange the toadstools on a bed of cress or shredded lettuce.

Fairy Necklaces

Thread pink and white marshmallows onto a string or cord with a large-eyed needle and hang them round your neck.

Butterfly Sandwiches

These pretty little sandwiches can be cut into the shape of butterflies and decorated.

INGREDIENTS
- ◆ 8 slices white or brown bread ◆ butter for spreading ◆ sandwich filling such as: cottage cheese and chives, tuna and cucumber, sandwich spread, cream cheese ◆ small bunch of chives ◆ radishes ◆ 1 carrot, peeled and thinly sliced ◆ cucumber strips

1. Stamp out circles from each slice of bread using a pastry cutter. Cut 4 of the circles in half and set aside.
2. Spread the remaining 4 whole circles of bread with sandwich filling.
3. Press 2 halves of bread in the centre of each at an angle for wings.

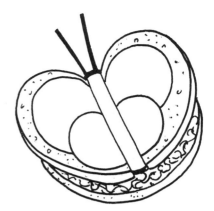

4. Lay a strip of cucumber down the middle of each sandwich for the body.

5. Arrange 2 pieces of chive at one end of each sandwich for antennae. Decorate the top of the wings with slices of cucumber, radish and carrot and serve.

PRETTY PEPPERMINTS

These peppermints are easy to make and with a few drops of food colouring can be made into a range of pretty pastel colours.

INGREDIENTS

- 250g/10 oz icing (confectioners') sugar
- 1 small egg (white only) ◆ a few drops peppermint essence
- few drops of red, blue, green food colouring ◆ 75g/3oz plain chocolate

1. To separate the egg, crack the shell and empty onto a plate. Turn an egg cup upside down over the yolk and, holding it firmly, tilt the plate over a mixing bowl so that only the egg white runs into the bowl.

2. Beat the egg white with a whisk until it is stiff.

3. Sieve the sugar into the egg white, a tablespoonful at a time. Mix well.

4. When you have added three-quarters of the sugar, pour in 6 drops of peppermint essence. Mix well and taste. Add more if necessary.

5. Continue adding the sugar until the mixture is no longer sticky. Knead it into a soft ball.

6. Divide the ball into three. Add a few drops of different food colouring to each ball, and knead in well.

7. Sprinkle a little icing sugar on a board. Put the ball on the board and press it out flat with your hands, until it is about 1/4" thick. Cut out the peppermints with a small round sweet cutter.

8. Arrange the peppermints on a piece of waxed paper sprinkled with icing sugar. Leave overnight until the peppermints are crisp.

9. Break the chocolate into pieces and place in a heatproof basin over a pan of gently simmering water until melted – ask an adult to help you. Remove from the heat and half-dip some of the peppermints in the chocolate. Place on the waxed paper and allow to set before serving.

Flower template
for paper daisy

ANSWERS

A Nature Crossword

1 *down* : buttercup
2 *across*: autumn
3 *across*: strawberry
4 *down*: rose
5 *across*: daisy
6 *down*: yellow

Spot the Difference

1. A flower is missing on the top left hand side
2. Some of the fairy's wing markings are missing
3. The strap of the bugle is coloured black
4. Part of the strap on the bugle horn is missing
5. The ties of the strap under the bugle horn are missing
6. The lip of the bugle horn is missing
7. The ribbons on the fairy's left slipper are missing
8. A leaf by the fairy's face is missing

Jumbled Words

EROS - Rose
TEWES APE - Sweet Pea
RIAMGLOD - Marigold
PILUT - Tulip